Day is yawning.
Quiet settles in the trees.
The birds fold their wings,
the singing stops.

Yellow sinks behind the rooftops.
A little boy watches the last drips of light
drop down on to long shadows.
Plop!

But what is
he holding?
Is it a key?

"It's time for bed, Max,"
his mother calls softly.

But Day is sleepy.
The milk-white daisies
droop and close,
a bank of tiny ghosts.

Two eyes,
two ears,
two wings,
wait,

as Day inches like a snail,

around the clock,

tick-tock,

tick-tock.

In the kitchen the spoons stop clinking. *Goodnight*, they wink to the kettle.

Everything waits.

The long window waits for the heavy drapes,
the bare wall waits for a shadow,
a bed waits for a boy,

a lock waits . . .
for a key!

Max smiles, for he knows it is time and the waiting is done.
Gently, he turns the key in the Night Box.

Click . . .
and another
click . . .

Up comes the lid . . .

WHOOSH!

Day slips inside as Night sweeps out.

Darkness tumbles into the air.
It dances and whirls around the room.
It goes under the bed, under the chair —
everywhere!

Hello, Night! laughs Max.

Night is mischievous!
It chases blue, white, pink, and green away.

Max presses his ear to the darkness. Night turns tiny sounds up LOUD.

Just a plink!
That's all.
Just a drip, not a waterfall!

Just a tap on the windowpane.
Just a little branch as gentle as rain, nothing more.

Just the tinkle of a bell
then a prrrrr —
not a lion! It's a kitten!

Max holds on tight as darkness swirls and spills
like ink into the world.
Night is huge. It can hold a house.
And a pond, and a forest.

A mountain, and a whale, even an ocean too!

Night soars, streams, stretches
up to the sky like a kite
and suddenly a thousand stars
sparkle and fizz, shine and spin.
This way, they say to a swan.
Where is she going?
She beats her strong white wings
and honks one word —
home.

Night is gentle. It floats down
to the ground like a feather.
It covers a fawn, asleep with her mother.
Night is brave.
Leave them in peace, Night warns.

Night shakes itself into the trees.

Come, badger!

Come, mole!

Come, owl!

Come, fox!

Let's play!

And out of the shadows they
snout and snuffle, leap and swoop.

Night gives a moon to a pond.
And a mole to a goose!
Now a rose has a fox.
And a kitten? She has the milk!

Everything has something in the dark.
The branch has an owl, and the wall has a tree,
and Max has a bear and a soft, warm bed.

Night is kind.
Night stays in Max's room,
silent and strong all night long,
to hold in its arms a bear and a boy.

But Night gets sleepy too.
Goodnight, me,
it sighs to itself.
My job is done.
It is time to return.

And when Night falls asleep . . .

Max opens the box and WHOOSH!
Night slips inside as Day sweeps out.

Day breathes into the leaves,
quiet flies out of the trees,
yellow rises from the rooftops,
and a new song begins.